One Sheep, Two Sheep

★ A book of collective nouns ★

To realising an idea—PB

For Tilly—TA

Little Hare Books
8/21 Mary Street, Surry Hills
NSW 2010 AUSTRALIA
www.littleharebooks.com

First published 2010

National Library of Australia
Cataloguing-in-Publication entry

Byers, Patricia.
One Sheep, Two Sheep/Patricia Byers; illustrator, Tamsin Ainslie.
9781921541452 (hbk.)
For pre-school age.
English language - Collective nouns - Juvenile literature.
Animals - Juvenile literature.
Ainslie, Tamsin.

425.54

Designed by Vida Kelly
Produced by Pica Digital, Singapore
Printed through Phoenix Offset
Printed in Shen Zhen, Guangdong Province, China, March 2010

5 4 3 2 1

One Sheep, Two Sheep

★ A book of collective nouns ★

By Patricia Byers

Illustrated by Tamsin Ainslie

LITTLE HARE
www.littleharebooks.com

One sheep,

two sheep,

a flock of sheep.

One lion,

two lions,

a pride of lions.

One goose,

two geese,

a gaggle of geese.

One elephant,

two elephants,

a parade of elephants.

One kangaroo,

two kangaroos,

a mob of kangaroos.

One frog,

two frogs,

a knot of frogs.

One mouse,

two mice,

a mischief of mice.

One butterfly,

two butterflies,

a kaleidoscope of butterflies.

One fish,

two fish,

a school of fish.

One child,

two children,

a party of children!